STANLEY IN SPACE

HarperTrophy®
An Imprint of HarperCollins Publishers

by Jeff Brown

Pictures by Scott Nash

**For Sidney Urquhart,
the godmother to whom Flat Stanley
owes so much.**

J
BROWN
JEFF

B-J
11/06

Harper Trophy® is a registered trademark of
HarperCollins Publishers Inc.

Stanley in Space

Text copyright © 1990 by Jeff Brown

Illustrations copyright © 2003 by Scott Nash

Library of Congress Cataloging-in-Publication Data

Brown, Jeff, 1926–

Stanley in space / by Jeff Brown ; pictures by Scott Nash.

    p.   cm.

    Summary: When the residents of a far-distant planet send a message to Earth asking
for someone to meet with them, the President of the United States asks Stanley
Lambchop, an all-American boy, to be his ambassador.

    ISBN 0-06-029827-8 (lib. bdg.) — ISBN 0-06-442174-0 (pbk.)

    [1. Space flight—Fiction.   2. Extraterrestrial beings—Fiction.   3. Heroes—Fiction.]

I. Nash, Scott, 1959– ill. II. Title.

PZ7.B81422 Su 2003   2002027560

[Fic]—dc21

First published in Great Britain 1990 by Methuen
Children's Books Ltd.

First Harper Trophy edition, 2003

Visit us on the World Wide Web!

www.harperchildrens.com

CONTENTS

"Will you meet with us?

Does anyone hear?"

From the great farness of space,

from farther than any planet or

star that has ever been mentioned

in books, the questions came.

Again and again.

"Will you meet with us?

Does anyone hear?"

THE CALL

It was Saturday morning, and Mr. and Mrs. Lambchop were putting up wallpaper in the kitchen.

"Isn't this nice, George?" said Mrs. Lambchop, stirring paste. "No excitement. A perfectly *usual* day."

Mr. Lambchop knew just what she meant.

3

Excitement was often troublesome. The flatness of their son Stanley, for example, after his big bulletin board settled on him overnight. Exciting, but worrying too, till Stanley got round again. And that genie visiting, granting wishes. Oh, very exciting! But all the wishes had to be *unwished* before the genie returned to the lamp from which he sprung.

"Yes, dear." Mr. Lambchop smoothed down wallpaper. "Ordinary. The very best sort of day."

In the living room, Stanley Lambchop and his younger brother, Arthur, were watching a Tom Toad cartoon on TV. The sporty Toad was water-skiing and fell off, making a great splash. Arthur laughed so hard he didn't hear the telephone, but Stanley answered it.

"Lambchop residence?" said the caller. "The President of the United States speaking. Who's this?"

Stanley smiled. "The King of France."

"They don't have kings in France. Not anymore."

"Excuse me, but I'm too busy for jokes." Stanley kept his eyes on the TV. "My brother and I are watching the Tom Toad Show."

"Well, you *keep* watching, young fellow!" The caller hung up, just as Mr. and Mrs. Lambchop came in to watch the rest of the show.

"Hey, guess what?" Stanley said.

"Hay is for horses," said Mrs. Lambchop, mindful always of careful speech. "Who called, dear?"

Stanley laughed. "The President of the United States!"

Arthur laughed too. "Stanley said *he* was the King of France!"

Tom Toad vanished suddenly from the TV screen, and an American flag appeared. "We bring you a special message from the White House in Washington, D.C.," said the deep voice of an announcer. "Ladies and gentlemen, the President of the United States!"

The screen showed the President, looking very serious, behind his desk.

"My fellow Americans," the President said. "I am sorry to interrupt this program, but someone out there doesn't realize that I am a very busy man who can't waste time joking

on the telephone. I hope the particular person I am talking to—and I do *not* mean the King of France!—will remember that. Thank you. Now here's The Toad Show again."

Tom Toad, still water-skiing, came back on the TV.

"Stanley!" exclaimed Mrs. Lambchop. "The King of France indeed!"

"Gosh!" Arthur said. "Will Stanley get put in jail?"

"There is no law against being a telephone

smarty," Mr. Lambchop said. "Perhaps there
should be."

The telephone rang, and he answered it.
"George Lambchop here."

"Good!" It was the President. "I've been

trying to get hold of you!"

"Oh, my!" Mr. Lambchop said. "Please excuse—"

"Hold on. You're the fellow has the boy was flat once, got his picture in the news-paper?"

"My son Stanley, Mr. President," Mr. Lambchop said, to let the others know who was calling.

"I had to be sure," said the President. "We have to get together, Lambchop! I'll send my private plane right now, fetch you all here to Washington, D.C."

Mr. Lambchop gasped. "Private plane? Washington? *All* of us?"

"The whole family." The President chuckled. "Including the King of France."

WASHINGTON

At the White House, in his famous Oval Office, the President shook hands with all the Lambchops.

"Thanks for coming." He chuckled. "Bet you never thought when you woke up this morning that you'd get to meet me."

"Indeed not," Mr. Lambchop said. "This is

quite a surprise."

"Well, here's another one," said the President. "The reason I asked you to come."

He sat down behind his desk, serious now. "Tyrra! Never heard of it, right?"

The Lambchops all shook their heads.

"*Nobody* ever heard of it. It's a planet, up there somewhere. They sent a message, the first ever from outer space!"

The Lambchops were greatly interested. "Imagine!" Mrs. Lambchop exclaimed. "What did it say?"

"Very friendly tone," the President said. "Peaceful, just checking around. Asked us to visit. Now, my plan—"

A side door of the Oval Office had opened suddenly to reveal a nicely dressed lady wearing a crown. Mrs. Lambchop recognized her at once as the Queen of England.

"About the banquet, also the—" the Queen began, and saw that the President was busy. "Ooops! We beg your pardon." She closed the door.

"This place is a *madhouse*," the President said. "Visitors, fancy dinners, no end to it. Now, where—? Ah, yes! The *Star Scout*!"

He leaned forward.

"That's our new top-secret spaceship, just ready now! Send somebody up in the *Star Scout*, I thought, to meet with these Tyrrans. But who? Wouldn't look peaceful to send soldiers, or even scientists. Then I thought: What could be more peaceful than just an ordinary American boy?"

The President smiled. "Why not Stanley Lambchop?"

"Stanley?" Mrs. Lambchop gasped. "In a spaceship? To meet with an alien race?"

"Oh, boy!" said Stanley. "I would love to go!"

"Me too," said Arthur. "It's not fair if—"

"Arthur!" Mr. Lambchop drew in a deep breath. "Mr. President, why *Stanley*?"

"It has to be someone who's already had adventure experience," the President said. "Well, my Secret Service showed me a newspaper story about when Stanley was flat and caught two robbers. Robbers! That's adventure!"

"I've had them too!" Arthur said. "A genie taught me to fly, and we had a Liophant, and—"

"A *what*?"

"A Liophant," Arthur said. "Half lion, half elephant. They're nice."

"Is that right? The Secret Service never—"

"Mr. President?" Mrs. Lambchop did not like to interrupt, but her concern was great.

"Mr. President?" she said. "This *mission*: Is it safe?"

"My goodness, of course it's safe!" the President said. "We have taken great care, Mrs. Lambchop. The *Star Scout* has all the latest scientific equipment. And it has been very carefully tested. First, we tried it on automatic pilot, with no passengers. It worked perfectly! Even then, ma'am, we were not satisfied. We sent the *Star Scout* up again, this time with our cleverest trained bird aboard. But hear for yourself." The President spoke into a little box on his desk. "Send in Dr. Schwartz, please."

A bearded man entered, wearing a white coat and carrying a birdcage with a cloth over it. Bowing, he removed the cloth to reveal a large, brightly colored parrot.

"Thank you, Herman," the President said. "Dr. Schwartz is our top space scientist," he told the Lambchops, "and this is Polly, the bird I spoke of. Polly, tell the folks here about your adventure into space."

"Piece of cake," said the parrot. "Terrific! Loved every minute of it!"

"Thank you, Herman," the President said, and Dr. Schwartz carried Polly away.

"That was very reassuring, but it is out of

the question for Stanley to go alone," Mrs. Lambchop said. "However, we *were* planning a family vacation. Would it be possible, Mr. President, for us all to go?"

"Well, if you didn't mind the crowding," the President said. "And skimping on baggage."

"Actually, we had in mind the seaside," Mr. Lambchop said. "Or a tennis camp. But—"

The Queen of England looked in again. "May we ask if—"

"Just a *minute*, for heaven's sake!" said the President.

"We shall return anon." Looking peeved, the Queen went away.

Mr. Lambchop had decided. "Mr. President, the seaside will keep. We will go

to Tyrra, sir."

"Wonderful!" The President jumped up. "To the stars, Lambchops! Some training at the Space Center, and you're on your way!"

TAKING OFF

"Ten!" said the voice of Mission Control.

The countdown had begun. When it reached "Zero" Chief Pilot Stanley Lambchop would press the "Start" button, and the *Star Scout* would blast off for Tyrra.

"Nine!"

Strapped into their seats, the Lambchops

held their breaths, each thinking very different thoughts.

Stanley was wondering if the Tyrrans would mind that Earth had sent just an ordinary family. Suppose they were big stuck-ups and expected a general or a TV star, or even the President? Suppose— "Eight!" said Control, and Stanley fixed his eyes on the panel before him.

Mr. Lambchop was thinking that serving one's country was noble, but this was a bit much. How did these things happen? Off to an unknown planet, the entire family! Other families didn't have a son become flat. Other families didn't find genies in the house. Other— Oh, well! Mr. Lambchop sighed.

"Seven!" said Control.

Mrs. Lambchop thought that Mr. Lambchop seemed fretful. But why, now that the *Star Scout* looked so *nice*? Thanks to her, in fact: "They may call it a spaceship," she had said when she first saw it, "but where's the *space*? Just one room! And all gray . . . ? Drab, I say!" Much of the training at the Space Center, however, was physical, and Mrs. Lambchop, who jogged and exercised regularly, quickly passed the tests required. In the days that followed, while the others were being made fit, she used her free time to make the *Star Scout* more like home. Only so much weight was permitted, but she managed a bathroom scale for the shower alcove and a plastic curtain, pretty shades for the portholes, a venetian blind for the Magnifying

Exploration Window, and posters of Mexico and France.

"Six! . . . Five! . . . Four! . . . Three! . . ."

Mrs. Lambchop made sure her purse was snug beneath her seat.

Arthur, by nature lazy, was thinking that he was glad to be done with all the jogging, jumping, climbing ladders, and scaling walls. When he was super-strong, thanks to the genie, it would have been easy. But for just plain Arthur Lambchop, he thought, it was tiring.

"Two!" said Control. "Good luck, everybody! One!"

"Pay attention, dear," Mrs. Lambchop told Stanley.

"Zero!" said Control, and Stanley pressed

the "Start" button.

Whrooom! Rockets roaring, the *Star Scout* rose from its launching pad.

Whroooooom! Whroooooom! Gaining speed, it soared higher and higher, carrying the Lambchops toward the farness where Tyrra lay.

IN SPACE

"I'll just flip this omelette," said Mrs. Lambchop, making breakfast in the *Star Scout*, "and then— Oh, dear!" The omelette hovered like a Frisbee in the air above her.

Mostly, however, after weeks in space, the

Lambchops remembered that gravity, the force that held things down, did not exist beyond Earth's atmosphere. Mr. Lambchop often read now with his hands clasped behind his head, allowing his book to float before him, and Stanley and Arthur greatly enjoyed pushing from their chairs to drift like feathers across the room.

Raising her pan, Mrs. Lambchop brought down the omelette. "After breakfast, what?" she said. "A game of Monopoly?"

"Please, not again." Arthur sighed. "If I'd known this adventure would be so boring, I'd never have come."

"The worst part," Stanley said, "is not knowing how long it will last."

"The beginning wasn't boring," Arthur

said as they began their breakfast. "The beginning was fun."

The first days had in fact been tremendously exciting. They had spent many hours at the *Star Scout*'s Magnifying Window, watching the bright globe of Earth grow steadily smaller, until it seemed at last only a pale marble in the black of space. And there had been many special sights to see: the starry beauty of the Milky Way, the planets— red Mars, giant Jupiter, cloudy Venus, Saturn with its shining rings.

The third evening they appeared on TV news broadcasts on Earth. Word of their voyage had been released to the press, and all over the world people were eager to learn how this extraordinary adventure was proceeding. Standing before the spaceship's camera, the Lambchops said they felt fine, looked forward to meeting the Tyrrans, and would report nightly while they remained in TV range.

The fourth evening they floated before the camera, demonstrating weightlessness. This was greatly appreciated on Earth, and they floated again the following day.

By the sixth evening, however, they were hard-pressed to liven their appearances. Mr. Lambchop recited a baseball poem, "Casey at the Bat." Stanley juggled tennis balls, but the Earth audience, knowing now about weightlessness, saw the balls float when he tossed

them up. Arthur did imitations of a rooster, a dog, and a man stuck in a phone booth. After this, while Mrs. Lambchop was singing her college song, he went behind the plastic curtain to undress for a shower and accidentally pulled the curtain down. He was mortified, and she tried later to comfort him.

"We will be remembered, Arthur, for our time in space," she said. "Nobody will care about a curtain."

"I will be remembered *forever*," Arthur said. "A hundred million people saw me in my underwear."

The next day was Stanley's birthday, and just after dinner the screen lit up. There was the President in his shirtsleeves, behind his desk in Washington, D.C.

"Well, here I am working late again," the President said. "It's a tough job, believe me. Happy birthday, Stanley Lambchop! I've arranged a surprise. First, your friends from school."

There was silence for a moment, broken only by the clearing of throats, and then, from all the millions of miles away, came the voices of Stanley's classmates singing, "Happy Birthday, dear Stanley! Happy Birthday to you!"

Stanley was tremendously pleased. "Thanks, everybody!" he said. "You too, Mr. President."

"That was just the U.S.A. part," said the President. "Ready over there in London, Queen?"

"We are indeed," the Queen's voice said cheerfully. "And now, Master Lambchop, our famous Westminster Boys' Choir!"

From England, the beautiful voices of the famous choir sang "Happy Birthday, Stanley!" all over again, and then other children sang it from Germany, Spain, and France.

All this attention to Stanley made Arthur jealous, and when the President said, "By the way, Arthur, you entertained us wonderfully the other night," he was sure this was a tease about his appearance in underwear. But he was wrong.

"Those imitations!" the President said. "Especially the fellow in the phone booth. Darn good!"

"Indeed!" the Queen added from England. "We were greatly amused."

"Oh, thank you!" said Arthur, cheered. "I—"

The screen had gone blank.

They had traveled too far. There would be no more voices from Earth, no voices but their own until they heard what the Tyrrans had to say.

"Suppose the Tyrrans have forgotten we're coming?" Stanley said. "We might just sail around in space *forever*."

They had finished the breakfast omelette, and were now setting out the Monopoly board because there was nothing more interesting to do.

"They don't even know our names," Arthur said. "What will they call us?"

"Earth people!" said a deep voice.

"Very probably," said Mr. Lambchop. "'Earth people' seems— Who said that?"

"Not me," said both Stanley and Arthur.

"Not *I*," said Mrs. Lambchop, correcting. "But who—"

"Earth people!" The voice, louder now, came from the *Star Scout*'s radio. "Greetings from the great planet Tyrra and its mighty people! Do you hear?"

"Oh, my!" Mr. Lambchop turned up the volume. "It's them!"

"They," said Mrs. Lambchop.

"For heaven's sake, Harriet!" Mr. Lambchop said, and spoke loudly into the microphone. "Hello, Tyrra. Earth people here. Party of four. Peace-loving family."

"Peace-loving?" said the voice. "Good! So is mighty Tyrra! Where are you, Earth people?"

Stanley checked his star maps. "We're just where the tail of Ralph's Comet meets star number three million and forty-seven. Now what?"

"Right," said the Tyrran voice. "Keep going till you pass a star formation that looks like a foot. You can't miss it. Then, just past a lopsided little white moon, start down. You'll see a pointy moun-

tain, then a big field. Land there. See you soon, Earth people!"

"You - bet!"

Mr. Lambchop said, and turned to his family. "The first contact with another planet! We are making history!"

They passed the foot-shaped star formation, then the lopsided moon, and Stanley piloted the *Star Scout* down. The darkness of space vanished as it descended, and at last the Lambchops saw clearly the planet it had taken so long to reach.

Tyrra was smallish as planets go, but nicely round and quite pretty, all in shades of brown with markings not unlike the oceans and continents of Earth. A pointy mountain came into sight, and beyond it a big field.

"There!" Stanley pressed the "Landing" button.

Whrooom! went the *Star Scout*'s rockets. The spaceship hovered, then touched down.

Peering out, the Lambchops saw only a brown field, with tan trees at the far side and brownish hills beyond.

"Curious," said Mr. Lambchop. "Where are—"

Suddenly a message came, but not the sort they expected.

"Surrender, Earth people!" said the radio. "Your spaceship is trapped by our unbreakable trapping cable! You are prisoners of Tyrra! Surrender!"

CHAPTER ·5·

THE TYRRANS

Unbreakable trapping cable? Prisoners? Surrender? The Lambchops could scarcely believe their ears.

"I don't call *that* peaceful," said Mrs. Lambchop. "Our President has been misled."

"I wish we had gone to the seaside." Mr. Lambchop shook his head. "But *how* are we trapped? I don't—" He pointed to the Magnifying Window. "What's that?"

A thin blue line, like a thread, had been passed over the *Star Scout*. Stanley switched on the wiper above the big window and the first flick of its blade parted the blue line.

"Drat!" said the radio.

Other voices rose, startled, and then the deep voice spoke again. "Earth people! We're sending a messenger! A regular, ordinary Tyrran, just to show what we're like."

For long moments, the Lambchops kept their eyes on the tan trees across the field.

"There!" Arthur said suddenly. "Coming toward— Oh! Oh, my . . ." His voice trailed away.

The Tyrran messenger came slowly forward to stand before the big window, a muscular, scowling young man with a curling mustache, wearing shorts and carrying a club.

The mustache was very large. The messenger was not.

"That man," Mrs. Lambchop said slowly, "is only three inches tall."

"At most," Mr. Lambchop said. "It is a magnifying window."

The Tyrran seemed to be calling something. Arthur opened the door a crack, and the words came clearly now. ". . . afraid to let us see you, Earth people? Because I'm so enormous? Hah! *All* Tyrrans are this big!"

Flinging the door wide, Arthur showed himself. "Well, I'm a *small* Earth person!" he shouted. "The rest are even bigger than me!"

"*I*, not me," Mrs. Lambchop said. "And don't tease, Arth— Oh! He's fainted!"

Wetting her handkerchief with cold water, she jumped down from the *Star Scout* and ran to dab the Tyrran's tiny brow.

Cries rose again from the spaceship's radio. "A giant killed Ik! . . . There's another, even bigger! . . . Oh, gross! . . . Look! Ik's all right!"

The Tyrran, by grasping Mrs. Lambchop's handkerchief, had indeed pulled himself up. Furious, he swung his club, but managed only to tap the top of her shoe. "Ouch! Scat!" she said, and he darted back across the field.

"Oh, my!" said the radio. "Never mind

about surrendering, Earth people! A truce committee is on the way!"

At first they saw only a tiny flag, fluttering like a white butterfly far across the brown field, but at last the Tyrran committee drew close, and the Lambchops, waiting now outside the *Star Scout*, could make each little person out.

The flag was carried by the scowling young man with the mustache and the club. The other members of the committee, a bit smaller even than he, were a red-faced man wearing a uniform with medals across the chest, a stout lady in a yellow dress and a hat with flowers on it, and two older men in blue suits, one with wavy white hair, the other thin and bald.

The committee halted, staring bravely up.

"I am General Ap!" shouted the uniformed man. "Commander of all Tyrran forces!"

Stanley stepped forward. "Chief Pilot Stanley Lambchop," he said. "From Earth. These are my parents, Mr. and Mrs. George Lambchop. And my brother, Arthur."

"President Ot of Tyrra, and Mrs. Ot," said General Ap, indicating the wavy-haired man and the lady. "The bald chap is Dr. Ep, our Chief

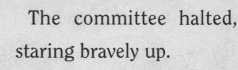

Scientist. The grouchy one with the flag is my aide, Captain Ik."

No one seemed sure what to say next. A few polite remarks were exchanged—"Nice meeting you, Earth people!" . . . "Such a pretty planet, Tyrra!" . . . "Thank you. Were you very long in space?"—and Mr. Lambchop realized suddenly that the Tyrrans were uncomfortable talking almost straight up. He got down on his knees, the other Lambchops following his example, and the Tyrrans at once lowered their heads in relief.

"Right!" said General Ap. "All reasonable people here! A truce, eh?"

"I'm for war, frankly," growled Captain Ik, but Stanley pretended not to hear. "A truce? Good idea," he said. "We come in peace."

Mrs. Ot sniffed. "Not very peaceful, frightening poor Captain Ik." She pointed at Arthur. "That giant shouted at him!"

"My son is not a giant," Mrs. Lambchop said. "It's just that you Tyrrans are—how to put it?—unusually *petite*."

"Ik's the biggest we've got, actually," said General Ap. "We hoped he'd scare you."

President Ot raised his hand. "No harm done! Come! TyrraVille, our capital, is but a stroll away."

The Lambchops, equipped now with handy magnifying lenses from the *Star Scout*'s science kit, followed the committee.

TyrraVille lay just across the brown field, behind the tan trees, no larger than an Earth-size tennis court.

TYRRAVILLE

"Gosh!" Stanley said. "It makes me home-sick, in a way."

Except for its size, and the lack of green-ness, the Tyrran capital was indeed much like a small village on Earth. A Main Street bustled with Tyrrans shopping and running errands; there were handsome school and public buildings, two churches with spires as high as Mr. Lambchop's waist, and side streets of pretty houses with lawns like neat brown postage stamps.

Captain Ik, still angry, marched on ahead, but the rest of the committee halted at the head of Main Street.

"We'll just show you *around*, eh?" said President Ot. "Safer, I think."

The Lambchops saw at once the risk of walking streets scarcely wider than their feet. Escorted by the committee, they circled the little capital, bending often to make use of their magnifying lenses. Mrs. Ot took care to indicate points of particular interest, among them Ux Field, a sports center, Admiral Ux Square, Ux Park, and the Ux Science Center

Building. ("Mrs. Ot's grandfather," whispered General Ap. "Very rich!")

The tour caused a great stir. Everywhere the tiny citizens of TyrraVille waved from windows and rooftops. At the Science Center, the last stop, journalists took photographs, and the Lambchops were treated to Grape Fizzola, the Tyrran national drink, hundreds of bottles of which were emptied into four tubs to make Earth-size portions.

Refreshed by his Fizzola, Arthur took a little run and hurdled a large part of TyrraVille, landing in Ux Square. "Arthur!" Mrs. Lambchop scolded, and he hurdled back.

"Aren't kids the dickens?" said a Tyrran mother, looking on. "Mine— Stop *tugging,* Herbert!" These last words seemed addressed

to the ground beside her. "My youngest," she explained.

Stanley squinted. "I can hardly— He's just a *dot*."

"Dot yourself!" said an angry voice. "Big-a-rooney! *You're* the funny-looking one!"

"Herbert!" his mother said. "It is rude to make fun of people for their shape or size!"

"As I said myself, often, when Stanley was flat!" Mrs. Lambchop exclaimed. "If only—"

"Surrender, Earth people!"

The cry had come from Captain Ik, who appeared now from behind the Science Center, staggering beneath the weight of a boxlike machine almost as big as he was, with a tube sticking out of it.

"Surrender!" he shouted. "You cannot resist our Magno-Titanic Paralyzer Ray! Tyrra will yet be saved!"

"There's a truce, Ik!" barked General Ap. "You can't—"

"Yes, I can! First— Ooops!" Captain Ik's knees had buckled, but he recovered himself. "First I'll paralyze the one who scared me back there in the field!"

Yellow light flickered up at Arthur from the Magno-Titanic Paralyzer.

"Yikes!" said Arthur, as shrieks rose from the crowd.

But it was not on Arthur that the Magno-Titanic beam landed. Stanley had sprung forward to protect his brother, and the light shone now on his chest and shoulders. Mrs. Lambchop almost fainted.

Suddenly her fright was gone.

Stanley was smil-ing. The yellow rays

still flickering upon him, he rolled his head and wiggled his hands to show that he was fine. "It's nice, actually," he said. "Like a massage."

The crowd hooted. "It only works on people Tyrran-size!" someone called. "You're a ninny, Ik!" Then Captain Ik was marched off by a Tyrran policeman, and the crowd, still laughing, drifted away.

Mrs. Lambchop spoke sternly to the committee. "'Tyrra will yet be saved'? What did Captain Ik mean? And why, pray tell, did he attempt to paralyze my son?"

The Ots and General Ap exchanged glances. Dr. Ep stared at the ground.

"Ah!" said President Ot. "Well . . . The fact is, we're having a . . . A crisis, actually. Yes.

And Ik, well, he, ah—"

"Oh, tell them!" Mrs. Ot burst suddenly into tears. "About the Super-Gro! Tell, for heaven's sake!"

Puzzled, the Lambchops stared at her. The sky had darkened, and now a light rain began to fall.

"Wettish, eh?" said General Ap. "Can't offer shelter, I'm afraid. No place large enough."

"The *Star Scout* will do nicely," said Mrs. Lambchop. "Let us return to it for tea."

CHAPTER ·7·

PRESIDENT OT'S STORY

"Tea *does* help. I am quite myself again." Mrs. Ot nodded to her husband. "Go on, dear. Tell."

Rain drummed faintly on the *Star Scout*, making even cozier the scene within. Around the dining table, the Lambchops occupied their usual places. The Tyrrans sat atop the table on thumbtacks pushed down to serve as stools, sipping from tiny cups Mrs. Lambchop had fashioned from aluminium foil, and nibbling crumbs of her homemade ginger snaps.

Now, sighing, President Ot set down his cup.

"You will have observed, Lambchops," he said, "how greatly we have enjoyed these tasty refreshments. The fact is, Tyrra has for some time been totally without fresh food or water fit to drink. We live now only by what tins and bottles we had in store."

Mrs. Ot made a face. "Pink meat spreads, and spinach. And that *dreadful* Fizzola."

"A bit sweet, yes," said General Ap. "Gives one gas, too. But—"

"Never mind!" cried Mrs. Ot.

President Ot continued. "The cause of our tragedy, Lambchops, was Super-Gro. An invention of Dr. Ep's. Super-Gro, Ep promised, would double our crops, make them double size, double delicious as well. A great concept, he said."

"We scientists," said Dr. Ep, "dream larger than other men."

"For three days, at the Science Center," President Ot went on, "Ep brewed his Super-Gro. Great smelly vats of it, enough for the whole planet. But then . . . Oh, no Tyrran will ever forget that fourth day! I myself was strolling through Ux Park. How beautiful it was! The trees and grass so green, the sky—"

"Green?" said Arthur. "But everything's *brown* here, not green!"

"A mishap," murmured Dr. Ep. "With the Super-Gro."

"Mishap?" barked General Ap. "The stuff *exploded*, Ep! All over the place!"

"Well, nobody's perfect." Dr. Ep hung his head.

"All those huge vats, Lambchops!" President Ot continued. "Boom! One after another! Shattered windows, blew the roof off the Science Center! No one hurt, thank goodness, but great clouds of smoke, darkening the sky! And then—such dreadful luck!—it began to rain. A *tremendous* rain, mixing with the smoke, falling all over Tyrra, into the rivers, on to every field and garden, every bit of greenery."

Rising from his thumbtack, he paced back and forth across the table.

"When the rain stopped, there was no green. None. Just brown. Worse, Ep's tests proved that our water was undrinkable, and that nowhere on Tyrra would anything grow. I broadcast at once to the nation. 'Do not despair,' I said, 'Tyrra will soon recover.'"

"Oh, good!" Mr. Lambchop said.

President Ot shook his head. "I lied. I couldn't tell the truth, for fear of causing panic, you see. The tests showed that it would be a year at least before Tyrra was green again. And long before that we will have emptied our last tin, our last bottle of Fizzola."

He sat down again, covering his face with his hands.

"So then we . . . We sent a message, into space. Lure some other planet's spaceship, we thought. Hold it for ransom, you see, make them send food and water. Oh, shameful! Underhanded. You will never forgive us, I know . . ."

His voice trailed away, and there was only the patter of the rain.

Close to tears, the Lambchops looked at each other, then at the little people on the tabletop. The Tyrrans seemed particularly tiny now, and brave, and nice.

"You poor dears!" Mrs. Lambchop said. "There was no need to *conquer* us. We would help you willingly, if we could."

The Tyrrans seemed at first unable to believe their ears. Then, suddenly, their faces shone with joy.

"Bless you!" cried General Ap.

"Saved!" Mrs. Ot clapped her hands. "We are saved!"

"Saved . . . ?" said Mrs. Lambchop.

"Of course!" said President Ot. "Don't you see? Earth's spaceships can bring food and water till— Oh! What's wrong?"

It was Arthur who explained.

"I'm very sorry," he said. "But there's just the *Star Scout*. Earth hasn't *got* any other spaceships. And it would take years to build them."

The Tyrrans gasped. "Years . . . ?" said Dr. Ep.

Stanley felt so sad he could hardly speak. "And it's no use going for food in the *Star Scout*," he said. "By the time we returned from Earth, you'd all be— Well, you know."

"Dead," said Mrs. Ot.

In the *Star Scout*, a terrible silence fell. The facts were clear. The cupboards of Tyrra would soon be empty. And then all its tiny people would starve to death.

STANLEY'S GOOD IDEA

The teapot was cold now, and a last cookie crumb lay unwanted on a plate. Gloom hung like a dark cloud within the *Star Scout*.

"It's not fair," Arthur said for the third time. "It's just not."

"Stop saying that," Stanley told him. "That's four times now."

"Five," said Dr. Ep.

General Ap tried to be cheerful. "Ah, well . . . Still some tinned meat, eh? And plenty of Grape Fizzola. Much to be thankful for."

"I will *never* be thankful for Grape Fizzola," said Mrs. Ot.

"It's just that . . ." Arthur sighed. "I mean, Earth has so *much* food. Millions of people, and there's mostly still enough."

The Tyrrans seemed amazed. "Millions? You're joking?" said President Ot.

"Hah!" said General Ap. "Dreadful crush, I should think. Millions?"

Mrs. Lambchop smiled. "With all our great nations, many millions. And still the numbers grow."

"Well, here too." President Ot shook his

head. "Youthful marriages, babies one after another. But *millions*? Our population—there's just TyrraVille, of course—is six hundred and eighty-three."

"Eighty-four," said Mrs. Ot. "Mrs. Ix had a baby last night."

Now it was the Lambchops who were amazed.

"Just TyrraVille?" Arthur cried. "But TyrraVille's your *capital*, you said!"

"Well, it would have to be, wouldn't it, dear?" said Mrs. Ot.

Stanley shook his head. "On the whole planet, only six hundred and eighty-four Tyrrans! Gosh, I'll bet— Wait!"

An idea had come to him. Stanley had had exciting ideas before, but none that excited him as this one did.

"Mrs. Ot!" he shouted. "How much do you weigh?"

"Stanley!" said Mrs. Lambchop.

Mrs. Ot was not offended. "Actually, I've slimmed a bit. Though not, sadly, in the hips. I'm six ounces, young man. Why do you ask?"

The words rushed out of Stanley. "Because if you're average, only children would be even lighter, then all the Tyrrans put together would weigh— Let me figure this out!"

"Less than three hundred pounds," said Mr. Lambchop, who was good at math. "Though I don't see—" Then he did see. "Oh! Good for you, Stanley!"

"The lad's bright, we know," said General Ap. "But what—"

"General!" said Mr. Lambchop. "Summon all Tyrrans here to the *Star Scout*! Fetch what remains of your tinned food and Grape Fizzola! Perhaps Earth can be your home till Tyrra is green again!"

THE
WEIGHING

From each little house on each little street, the Tyrrans came, every man, woman, and child, even Captain Ik with a guard from the jail. The rain had stopped, and the evening light shone gold on the brown field in which the tiny people stood assembled.

President Ot addressed them. "Fellow

Tyrrans! I must confess that your government has deceived you! The truth is: It will be at least a year before our fields and streams are fit again."

Cries rose from the crowd. "We were lied to!" . . . "Lordy, talk about bad news!" . . . "We'll starve!" . . . "Shoot the scientists!"

"Wait!" shouted President Ot. "We are offered refuge on Earth, if the voyage is possible! Pay attention, please!"

Stepping forward, Mr. Lambchop read aloud from the booklet that had come with the *Star Scout*.

"'Your spacecraft has been designed for safety as well as comfort. Use only as directed.'" He raised his voice. "'Do not add weight by bringing souvenirs aboard *or by inviting friends to ride with you.*'"

Cries rose again. "That did it!" . . . "We're not *souvenirs*!" . . . "He said no friends either, stupid!" . . . "We've had it, looks like!"

Mr. Lambchop raised his hand. "There is still hope! But you must all be weighed! Also the supplies you would require for the trip!"

The *Star Scout*'s bathroom scales, set down in the field, proved too high for the Tyrrans, and the weighing was briefly delayed until Arthur, using the Monopoly board, made a ramp by which they could easily mount.

General Ap barked orders. "Right, then! Groups of twenty to twenty-five, families together! And don't jiggle!"

The Ots and six other families marched up

onto the scale, beside which Mrs. Lambchop stood with pad and pencil. "Seven and one-quarter pounds!" she said, writing it down.

"Next!" shouted General Ap, but the Ot group was already starting down, and another marching up.

Group after group mounted the scale. There *was* jiggling, due to excited children, but Mrs. Lambchop took care to wait until the needle was still. Within an hour the entire population of Tyrra had been weighed, along with its supplies of tinned food and Fizzola, and she added up.

"Tyrrans, two hundred and thirty-nine," she announced. "Food and Fizzola, one hundred and forty. Total: Three hundred and seventy-nine pounds!"

"Are we saved? Or are we too fat?" came a cry.

"Too soon to tell!" Mr. Lambchop called back. "We must see how we can lighten our ship!"

A good start was made by discarding the *Star Scout*'s dining table and one steel bunk, since Stanley and Arthur could easily share. Then out went Stanley's tennis balls, extra sweater, and his Chief Pilot zip jacket with the American flag; out went Arthur's knee socks, raincoat, and a plastic gorilla he had smuggled aboard. Mr. and Mrs. Lambchop added their extra clothing, lamps, kitchen-ware, the Monopoly game, and at last, the posters of Mexico and France.

The crowd stood hushed as the pile was

weighed. Somewhere a baby cried, and its parents scolded it.

"Three hundred and seventy-seven pounds!" Mrs. Lambchop announced. "Oh, dear!" she whispered to President Ot. "Two less than we need."

"I see." President Ot, after a moment's thought, climbed up onto the scale. "Good news, Tyrrans!" he called. "Almost all of us are saved!"

Cheers went up, and then someone shouted, "What do you mean, *almost* all?"

"We weigh, as a nation, a bit too much," President Ot explained. "But only four, if largish, need stay behind. I shall be one. Will three more volunteer?"

Murmurs rose from the crowd. "That's *my*

kind of President!" . . . "Leave Ik behind!" . . . "How about you, Ralph?" . . . "Ask somebody else, darn you!"

The matter was quickly resolved. "I won't go without you, dear," Mrs. Ot told her husband, and Captain Ik, hoping to regain popularity, announced that he too would remain.

General Ap was the fourth volunteer. "Just an old soldier, ma'am," he told Mrs. Lambchop. "Lived a full life, time now to just fade away, to—"

"Hey! Wait!"

Arthur was pointing to the scale.

"We forgot *that*," he said. "We can leave the scale behind. Now nobody has to stay!"

HEADING HOME

"Mr. and Mrs. Ix, and the new baby?" said President Ot, beside his wife on a ledge above the Magnifying Window. "Ah, yes, on the fridge!"

The people of Tyrra were being made as comfortable as possible in the various nooks and crannies of the *Star Scout*. Stanley and

Arthur had cleared a cupboard where Tyrra High School students could study during the trip, and Mrs. Lambchop had cut up sheets to make hundreds of little blankets, and put out bits of cotton for pillows. "Makeshift, Mrs. Ix," she said now, settling the Ixes on the fridge. "But *such* short notice. Back a bit from the edge, yes?"

"Short notice indeed," said Mrs. Ix. "So many—"

"Not to worry." Mrs. Lambchop smiled proudly. "My son, the Chief Pilot, will call ahead."

From a nearby shelf, Captain Ik whispered an apology for attempting to paralyze Arthur. "Between you and I, I didn't really think it would work," he said.

"Between you and *me*," said Mrs. Lambchop. "But thank you, Captain Ik." She turned to Stanley. "We're all ready, dear!"

Stanley checked his controls. "Let's go!"

"Tyrrans!" President Ot called for attention. "Our national anthem!"

Everywhere in the *Star Scout*, Tyrrans rose, their right hands over their hearts. "*Hmmmm . . .*" hummed Mrs. Ot, setting a key, and they began to sing.

"Tyrra, the lovely! Tyrra, the free!

Hear, dear planet, our promise to thee!

Where e'er we may go, where e'er we may roam,

We'll come back to Tyrra, Tyrra our home!"

The words echoed in the softly lit cabin.

Many Tyrrans were weeping, and the eyes of the Lambchops, as they took their seats, glistened too.

"Be it ever so humble, there's no planet so dear,

We'll always love Tyrra, from far or from—"

Stanley pressed the "Start" button, and—

Whroooom!—the *Star Scout*'s rockets roared to life.

The singing stopped suddenly, and Mrs. Ix cried out from the fridge. "Oh, my! Is this thing safe?"

"Yes indeed," Mrs. Lambchop called back.

"Perhaps," said Mrs. Ix. "But it is my belief that if Tyrrans were meant to fly, we'd have wings."

Whroooom! Whroooom!

The *Star Scout* lifted now, gaining speed as it rose. Its mission was done. The strangers who had called from a distant planet were no longer strangers, but friends.

It was all very satisfactory, Stanley thought. The other Lambchops thought so too.

CHAPTER
·11·

EARTH AGAIN

". . . real pleasure to welcome you, Tyrrans," said the President, almost done with his speech. "I wish you a fine year on Earth!"

Before him on the White House lawn, with newspaper and TV reporters all about, sat the Lambchops and, in a tiny grandstand built especially for the occasion, the people of Tyrra.

The Tyrrans were now applauding politely, but they looked nervous, and Mrs. Lambchop guessed why. That crowd at the Space Center for the *Star Scout*'s landing, that drive through crowded streets into Washington, D.C.! Poor Tyrrans! Everywhere they looked, giant buildings, giant people. How could they feel comfortable here?

But a surprise was in store. Across the lawn, a great white sheet had been spread. Now, at the President's signal, workmen pulled the sheet away.

"Welcome," said the President, "to TyrraVille Two!"

Gasps rose from the Tyrrans, then shouts of joy.

Before them, on what had been the White House tennis court, lay an entire village of tiny houses, one for each Tyrran family, with shops and schools and churches, and a miniature railway serving all principal streets. Begun when Stanley called ahead from space, TyrraVille Two had been completed well before the *Star Scout*'s arrival, thanks to rush deliveries from leading toy stores in Washington and New York.

The excited Tyrrans ran from the grandstand to explore their new homes, and soon happy voices rose from every window and doorway of TyrraVille Two. "Nice furniture!" . . . "Hooray! Fresh lemonade! No more Fizzola!" . . . "In the cupboards, see? Shirts, dresses, suits, shoes!" . . . "Underwear, even!"

The Ots, General Ap, Dr. Ep, and Captain Ik came back to say good-bye, and the Lambchops knelt to touch fingertips in farewell. The TV men filmed this, and Arthur made everyone laugh, pretending to be paralyzed by the touch of Captain Ik. Then the newsmen left, the Tyrrans returned to TyrraVille Two, and only the President remained with the Lambchops on the White House lawn.

"Well, back to work." The President sighed. "Good-bye, Lambchops. You're all heroes, you know. Saved the nation."

"Not really," Stanley said. "They couldn't have conquered us."

"Well, you know what I mean," the President said. "You folks care to stay for supper?"

"Thank you, no," Mrs. Lambchop said. "It is quite late, and this has been an exciting but very tiring day."

It was bedtime when they got home. Stanley and Arthur had a light supper, with hot chocolate to help them sleep, after which Mr. and Mrs. Lambchop tucked them in and said good night.

The brothers lay quietly in the darkness for a moment. Then Arthur chuckled.

"The Magno-Titanic Paralyzer *was* sort of scary," he said. "You were brave, Stanley, protecting me."

"That's okay," Stanley said. "You're my brother, right?"

"I know . . ." Arthur was sleepy now.

"Stanley? When the Tyrrans go back, will their land and water be okay? Will they let us know?"

"I guess so." Stanley was drowsy too. "Good night, Arthur."

"Good night," said Arthur, and soon they were both asleep.

And in time, from the great

farness of space, but a farness no

longer strange or unknown,

another message came.

"We are home. All is well."

And again.

"We are home! Thank you, Earth!

All is well!"